GHOST EYE

GHOST EYE

MARION DANE BAUER

ILLUSTRATED BY
TRINA SCHART HYMAN

AN
APPLE
PAPERBACK

SCHOLASTIC INC.
New York Toronto London Auckland Sydney

ISBN 0-590-45299-1

Text copyright © 1992 by Marion Dane Bauer. Illustrations copyright © 1992 by Trina Schart Hyman. All rights reserved. Published by Scholastic Inc. APPLE PAPERBACKS is a registered trademark of Scholastic Inc.

12 11 10 9 8 7 6 5 4 3 2 1   11   4 5 6 7 8 9/9

For
Meghan and *Jessica Guernsey*
with special love,
and for the real *Purrloom Popcorn* of course!

— M. D. B.

Contents

GHOST EYE

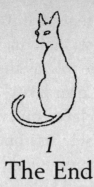

1

The End

EVERYONE loved Purrloom Popcorn.

He was, after all, a unique cat, a white Cornish rex with one eye of brilliant blue and one of shining gold. His short, soft coat formed deep waves all over his sleek body. His head was chiseled to a fine wedge. His delicately veined ears were enormous. His tail was long, so long that, when sitting, he could wrap it across both front ankles and still have an inch left over to curl or twitch as he chose.

Other cats who competed in the shows always had to work to get people to notice them, but not Popcorn. Cross-faced Persians tried to smile. Normally aloof Siamese purred. Kittens tumbled and wrestled with one another, advertising their cuteness. But Popcorn merely sat on the highest shelf in his cage, gazing solemnly at the people as they passed by.

"Look at that Cornish rex!" they would say to one another. "Have you ever seen anything so extraordinary? He has one eye of brilliant blue and one of shining gold."

And Popcorn would blink first his blue eye, then his gold, and they would all draw in their breaths. "How wonderful!" they would cry.

The judges thought Popcorn was wonderful, too. In show after show, he was declared Best of Color, Best of Breed, Best Cat in his ring, and over and over again, Best of the Best.

His agents, the changing stream of people who attended him at shows, were pleased to be in charge of a Grand Champion. They fed him only the highest quality kitty kibbles and kept his water fresh and cool and polished his coat with the softest chamois.

They rarely cuddled him, however, and never tickled his curly whiskers and, since he wasn't their cat, they wouldn't have dreamed of taking him home to sleep at the foot of the bed.

Popcorn didn't mind. He was, after all, above the comforts and pleasures of mere house cats. He had ribbons adorning the walls of his cages (a small cage for shows, a larger one at the cattery), and he was admired by humans and envied by other cats. He had even, on one occasion, been featured on the cover of *The Distinctive Cat*, a magazine for cat lovers.

Once, long ago, Popcorn, himself, had been a house cat. He had lived in a very large house with an old woman named Lydia. But that had been when he was a small kitten and before he was a Grand Champion. And it was also before Lydia had grown ill and been sent to a place where cats, even Grand Champions, weren't allowed.

"Don't worry, Popcorn," she had told him. "You'll be well cared for, and we'll be back together again in just a little while."

But the "little while" had stretched into a long one, and Lydia hadn't called for him. Popcorn sat on the lowest shelf of his cage in the cattery, his long tail drooping and his eyes dull.

"This cat needs more attention!" the man who owned the cattery said, and he turned Purrloom Popcorn over to an agent who began entering him in shows.

At show after show, Popcorn peered past his growing collection of ribbons to check the crowds. Would he see Lydia? Had she come? Sometimes he caught a glimpse of a colorful dress or heard a quavering voice call, "kitty-kitty-kitty," and his heartbeat quickened. But the dress or the voice never turned out to belong to *his* old woman, and gradually he quit studying the crowds, quit caring about all the not-Lydias who flocked around his cage. Gradually, he even forgot her name or that there had been a time when he had loved a human.

There were dreams occasionally, of gentle hands, a warm lap, tidbits of fresh fish nibbled from gnarled fingers. But the dreams slipped away each time he awoke, leaving behind only a trace of sadness. To banish the sadness, Popcorn had only to close his blue eye and look out through the gold one with a long, steady stare. Somehow, the world always seemed more solid that way. Besides . . . what reason could he possibly have to be sad? He was loved and admired everywhere he went.

Then one day he overheard the man who owned the cattery talking to his latest agent. "I just got word," he said. "Lydia has died."

Lydia? Died? Something deep inside Popcorn trembled. But still he couldn't quite remember who Lydia had been. Was she the judge who'd awarded him five blue ribbons last year? Or was she one of his former agents, the one who'd always told him he was the most beautiful Cornish rex she'd ever seen? Confusion struggled with sorrow, but Popcorn had no idea what there was to be sorrowful about.

"The will has been read," the man went on, taking Popcorn from his cage and putting him into the one he used for travel, "and all her cats are to be sent home."

Home! Popcorn hooked his curving claws through the wire of the cage wall. *HOME!!!* What home did he have except for his comfortable cages, the succession of shows, the judges' tables? What life did he have except for his adoring fans, the ever-accumulating ribbons, the lights, and the glory?

"No!" he cried as the cover dropped over his cage. "You can't send me away!" he cried again in the smothering darkness.

But humans are quite limited in their ability to understand, and even if the man had known what Popcorn was saying, he had little choice. He had received his orders.

When Popcorn felt his cage being picked up, he huddled in the corner and squeezed both of his eyes shut, the fine blue and the gleaming gold. Maybe, he said to himself, he would just keep them shut for the rest of his life. Who, after all, would know enough to appreciate an odd-eyed Cornish rex in this strange place called home?

Clearly, the good life had come to an end.

2
The Arrival

MELINDA sat on the front steps of the rambling old house. The steps were long, the porch that loomed behind her, immense, the front door, much taller, wider, thicker than a door needed to be just for letting people in and out. Even the trees in the yard stretched up and up until they seemed to be trying to scrape against the sky. All of that largeness made Melinda feel extremely small, sitting there. But there was nothing she could do about that.

When Great-aunt Lydia had died, she had left the house and the steps and the porch and the front door and the trees to Melinda's father and to Melinda's mother and, whether she wanted any of it or not, to Melinda. In fact, Great-aunt Lydia had left Melinda's family everything she owned, including Purrloom Popcorn, the only one of her cats to outlive her.

Melinda didn't much care about the dusty furniture, which her parents said was antique. She didn't even care about the money, which her father said was "quite sufficient." The only thing she cared about was Purrloom Popcorn, whom she had yet to meet. He had been living in a cattery during Lydia's long illness and had even traveled around the country winning ribbons in shows. ("Quite an expensive business," her father had said.) But now he was coming home.

"It's a small price to pay," Melinda's parents had told her, "being guardians to one of that strange woman's cats, in exchange for this grand, old house."

Melinda had hardly been able to believe her luck. She had wanted a cat for almost as long as she could remember, but her parents, as they had often explained, weren't particularly fond of cats.

So, with barely a backward glance, she had left her small, sunny room in her small, sunny house. Without a single complaint, she had moved away from her neighborhood and her friends and her school. And now, on a pale, spring afternoon, she sat on the front steps of the too-big, too-old house, waiting for Purrloom Popcorn to appear. It was a large price to pay, giving up her entire world, but worth it in exchange for her very own cat!

When a car pulled up in front of the house and a man climbed out, carrying the covered cage, Melinda leapt to her feet. "Popcorn's here!" she called to her parents. "Come see!"

But her mother was painting the kitchen and her father was sorting out closets, and neither of them came. "You take care of it, dear," they both called. It was only a cat, after all. Surely Melinda could manage that.

And of course, Melinda could, though the agent grumbled about turning a cat of such fine pedigree over to a child. She listened carefully as the agent gave her instructions. No rich food lest Purrloom Popcorn put on weight. No drafts lest he catch a chill. Not too much handling lest his delicate coat be damaged.

Then the agent muttered his way back to his car, and Melinda carried the cage inside.

What does he know? she thought. *I'll feed my cat whatever he likes and leave the windows open so he can talk to the birds and hug and pet him night and day. That's the proper way to care for a cat!* Then she uncovered the cage.

For a long time she stared at the strange creature she saw inside. He didn't look like a cat. He was too long, too skinny, too wrinkled, and he had too little fur. And besides all that, he sat in the corner of the cage with his eyes closed tight like a mole. Was this what a Cornish rex cat was supposed to look like?

She gently shook the cage. Popcorn's eyes flew open — almost in spite of himself, it seemed — and she gasped and put one hand over her mouth to suppress a giggle. "No wonder Great-aunt Lydia liked you," she said.

"Your eyes don't match! Nothing ever matched about her, either."

Popcorn scowled at the girl. So this was the human who had dared to call him "home"! There was nothing particularly distinctive about her, that was for certain. She was medium-sized, with dark eyes (both of them quite boringly the same) and dark, curling hair. Not neat, close-fitting waves such as his, but a tangled mop of individual curls.

The girl scowled back at him. "You're the funniest-looking cat I ever saw!" she said.

Funny-looking! So it was going to be even worse than he had feared. Not only was this girl ignorant about cats, especially Cornish rex, particularly Grand Champions, but she was rude as well.

Then she did something which proved how little she knew. She opened the cage door. A valuable cat such as he was never allowed to wander about loose. However, since the girl obviously didn't know any better, Popcorn decided to take advantage of the moment. He poked his head out the open door and peered around.

The place was almost big enough for a cat show, though there were no signs that a show was in progress or even planned. He rippled his skin nervously, but still he stepped out. After all, he wasn't going to have this child thinking he was afraid.

He examined the distant ceiling, the windows arching toward the sky, and sat down and wrapped his tail about himself snugly. It was a comforting thing, a tail. Almost as comforting as the familiar walls of his cage.

The girl walked all around him, staring. "Weird," she said finally, shaking her dark curls.

Popcorn gave her his most disgusted look, the one he usually reserved for judges with cold hands. What a terrible job humans did of training their young! Then he turned away from the girl and began washing one pink and white paw. That would show her how little he cared about the opinions of an ill-bred child.

Cautiously, Melinda reached a hand out and ran it down Popcorn's back. He was curly! Why, even his whiskers twisted this way and

that. And though he was velvety soft to her touch, she had never seen a cat with such outsized ears or so little fur.

Great-aunt Lydia had always had lots of cats. Why couldn't the one left for them to inherit have been normal, with two green eyes and lots of straight, multi-colored fur?

She stroked Popcorn again, but he stood and moved away. Then he sat down again, just beyond her reach, and stretched his neck to wash away her touch.

Melinda didn't need Popcorn's agent to explain what *that* meant. The cat didn't like her. The cat she'd been dreaming of for practically her entire life didn't want anything to do with her!

Slowly she stood up. Slowly she walked to the door. Then she turned back to check Popcorn again. He sat there, his face screwed into a prolonged and ridiculous-looking wink, watching her out of his gold eye.

He wasn't fooling her, though. She knew he was odd-eyed. As far as she was concerned, he was odd everything. And stuck-up on top of it all. He certainly wasn't a cat to trade a home, a neighborhood, a school, friends, a world for!

She stepped onto the porch and closed the door behind herself, hard. What reason was there now for staying? Certainly Purrloom Popcorn wasn't going to care if she ran away.

And, of course, she was right. Popcorn didn't care. He watched her go without the slightest twinge of pity or even interest. After she had shut the door, he merely turned to examine the room again.

If this was supposed to be the place he'd come from . . . well, he couldn't say that he remembered it or would have had any reason to want to. The Civic Center in St. Paul, where he had attended shows three years in a row, was grander . . . and more familiar, too.

He turned to go back into his cage, but stopped at the door. It seemed small, somehow, after the brief freedom of the room. And the idea of sitting in that enclosure, waiting for someone to show up to admire him didn't really appeal. There didn't seem to be anyone here whose opinion was of much consequence, anyway.

So Purrloom Popcorn lashed his tail, sharpened his claws on the lush velvet of a nearby chair, and set out to explore the old house instead.

Still, he wondered, how could this Lydia, whoever she had been, have betrayed him so?

3
The Discovery

AFTER Melinda left Great-aunt Lydia's house, she walked. She walked until her feet hurt. She walked until she had almost forgotten her way back. She walked until the sun began playing peekaboo behind some of the taller trees. Then, finally, she stopped.

What was the point of running away? And where was she running to? Another family would be living in her little house. Someone else would have her desk at school as well. And Meghan and Jessica, her two best friends, would probably be so busy playing with one another that they would have forgotten her already.

Sadly, Melinda retraced her steps toward Great-aunt Lydia's house and the old woman's disappointing cat. When she got there, she wasn't going to go inside, though. Not yet. Let them worry! Let them all worry.

Back at the house, however, her parents were too busy painting and sorting to worry. And Popcorn wouldn't have worried anyway, but he was also busy. He had found his way to Melinda's room on the second floor, though he neither knew nor cared whose room it was that he had found. What he was actually interested in was the open window he had discovered and the gaping hole torn in the window screen by a branch from a close-standing tree.

He sat on the windowsill and poked his head through the hole. The perfect escape! He had only to decide where he wanted to escape to!

San Antonio? New Orleans? Seattle? Cincinnati? He had visited them all and had won blue ribbons in every one. Phoenix? Miami? Providence? Milwaukee? What about Los Angeles? The truth was, Popcorn knew nothing of the many cities he had been in except for the insides of the local cat shows. So one place was exactly like another to him. But if he could get himself out of this terrible house, he was determined to go *somewhere* where he would find another show.

He stretched a tentative paw through the hole in the screen, prepared to step out onto the branch. Or almost prepared. He tapped the branch lightly, then hesitated, his paw suspended in the air.

Popcorn, of course, had never climbed a tree before. He had never, in fact, been any higher than the tallest shelf in his cage. And this slender, roughly coated branch didn't look nearly as reliable as his carpeted shelf, not to mention being considerably farther from the ground.

If the branch didn't hold him, if he didn't cling tightly enough, if he made the slightest misstep, the drop would be enough to curl a cat's whiskers . . . even if that cat's whiskers hadn't already been curled, which, of course, his were.

He turned back, muttering a few swear words like "dog's breath" and "bath," and jumped to the bed. A stuffed, pink kitten was lying on the pillow, and Popcorn gave the thing a cuff. Who ever heard of a cat with pink fur, anyway? A freak like that would be barred from shows. Then he dropped to the floor. There had to be another way out of this place.

Halfway down the stairs, he stopped. There was something barring his way that hadn't been there when he'd come up. Whatever it was, it almost blended into the shadowy stairs. Popcorn peered intently first with his gold eye and then with his blue before the figure came clear.

It was a cat stretched across the bottom step, an enormous ginger tabby. Definitely not a show cat. Why, anyone could see at a glance that the old tom was as common as kitty litter. One ear even had several deep notches, the sure mark of a brawler.

At first Popcorn considered walking right on past the creature without speaking. He certainly wasn't interested in holding a conversation with a lowlife such as this. But walking past was exactly the problem, as the ginger tom occupied most of the step.

"Excuse me, my good cat," Popcorn said as politely as he could without, of course, being the least bit familiar. "Would you mind if I pass?"

"The name's Tiger," the tom replied. "And you can do anything you want, chum." However, having said that, he stretched out even farther until a creamy paw touched one end of the step and his striped tail reached to the other. (It was, Popcorn couldn't help noting, a rather stubby tail. Probably worth no more than two points in a show. Popcorn's long, tapering appendage always brought down the full five.) But then Tiger added with a warning growl, "Just don't wiggle my whiskers on your way by."

Popcorn looked at the large tabby's whiskers. They were — even he had to admit it — magnificently long. They also looked very much in the way. And if Popcorn did manage to get past without brushing against them, the old cat would probably wiggle his whiskers himself to guarantee a fight.

Purrloom Popcorn had exchanged hisses through the walls of his cage with the best of them, but he had never unsheathed his claws in an actual fight. He had once known a Manx who had taken on a street-smart Russian blue. The Manx had been left so scarred he'd been forced to retire from the show circuit.

"Look, Tiger," he said, doing his best to remain reasonable and calm, "if this is your house, you're welcome to it. I'm just looking for a way out, myself. In fact, I'm on my way to a show in Des Moines."

"A showboy, huh?" Tiger sneered, curling his upper lip to reveal long yellow teeth. "No wonder you're so purty."

Popcorn wasn't quite sure why, but having this ruffian say he was "purty" was worse than being called "funny-looking" by the girl. And though he knew it made no sense to provoke the beast, he couldn't help it. He twitched his tail and arched his neck, just a bit.

Tiger didn't bother to rise in response to the challenge. But he ran his tongue over the tip of his nose, one small lick.

Popcorn knew alley language, at least enough to read the danger signals. He even considered retreating up the steps. He was

25

aware, though, that there was no escape route behind him except for the hole in the screen . . . and the abyss beyond. What would he do if this obnoxious fellow followed him upstairs?

The big tom stood now, slowly, menacingly. He flared his ears until his head was as broad and as flat as a shelf. His tongue flicked out to touch his nose again.

Spit in your eye! Popcorn thought, but he didn't say it, let alone do it. And before he could decide whether to attack or take his chances on retreat, Tiger lifted a massive paw, claws extended like rapiers, and slashed at the side of his face.

The blow missed, which was odd at such close range. Popcorn felt only a cool wind across his left cheek. But stranger still, when he closed his eye against the descending claws — it happened to be the blue one — he found himself staring into empty space.

The bullying tom had disappeared entirely.

Popcorn blinked, and instantly the other cat was back. "Where'd you go?" he demanded to know.

"Go?" Tiger snorted. "I ain't gone no-where. You're the one ducked out of the fight."

Popcorn hadn't ducked. He knew that. He had done no more than close his blue eye. Still, he decided not to argue the point. "Look," he tried instead. "If you'll just show me how to get out of this place, I'll be on my way to Albuquerque. And I won't bother you again. Believe me."

"What's to show?" Tiger shrugged, and the muscles rippled beneath his tawny fur. "You just leave."

To himself Popcorn thought, *This fellow must not be very bright*. But he explained patiently, "The door's shut. Can't you see? The girl closed it behind her when she went out."

"Door?" Tiger scratched one side of his chin until puffs of ginger fur flew. "You want to go out through a door?" He gave Popcorn a puzzled look, as though a door were a strange means of exit. But then he shrugged again. "So long as you go, I guess it don't matter how. Follow me."

He headed for the door, and Popcorn followed eagerly. Now that he'd thought of finding his own way to Philadelphia for his next cat show, he didn't want to waste another minute inside this old house.

The massive wooden door was, as he had already pointed out to Tiger, tightly closed. But perhaps there was some way past it that he hadn't noticed.

Tiger swaggered on toward the door, his head high. He might have been expecting a servant to appear and open it for him. No servant materialized, though, and the door remained shut.

Despite that fact, Tiger didn't hesitate, even for an instant. To Popcorn's profound astonishment, he simply walked right through the closed door and disappeared on the other side.

It was as though the heavy, wooden door — or perhaps the cat himself — were no more solid than smoke.

4
The Escape

POPCORN was still standing in the middle of the vestibule, gaping, when Tiger returned. The ginger tom passed back through the wall as effortlessly as he had gone out through the closed door.

"How . . . how did you do that?" Popcorn stammered.

"Do what?" Tiger asked. He sat down and began to scrub his flaring whiskers. It was obvious that the old fellow was fully aware of just how spectacular they were.

"How did you go out through the door? How did you come back through the wall?"

Tiger stopped washing and stared at Popcorn, his amber eyes round. "You ain't much of a spook, are you," he said, "asking a dumb question like that!"

"Spook?" If he could have grown more white, Popcorn would have. "What are you talking about?"

"Phantom, spirit, ghost," Tiger continued in an irritable way, as though he found Popcorn dense.

Popcorn shivered. "I'm . . . I'm not. Any of those things."

"What are you then?" the other cat asked, narrowing his eyes.

"I'm *alive*," Popcorn replied, almost apologetically.

Tiger stepped closer. He sniffed, then wrinkled his nose in distaste. "Fish bones," he said. "You even smell alive. Why didn't I notice before?"

Popcorn said nothing, but he was feeling a bit faint. Was it possible, could it be that he was talking to a *ghost*?

Then Tiger pressed his face so close to Popcorn's that the Cornish rex almost fell over backwards. "What I want to know," Tiger growled, "is how come you can see me. Most breathing folks can't."

"I . . . I don't have any idea," Popcorn gasped.

Tiger stared even harder, then suddenly pulled back. "Oh, I get it!" he exclaimed. "You've got a ghost eye, too!"

"A what?" Popcorn gasped, thoroughly bewildered. And what did the fellow mean by *too*? Besides being handsome, besides being impeccably bred, besides being a Grand Champion, he had a . . . "What did you say I have?" he asked.

"A ghost eye," Tiger repeated. "That funny-looking blue one. It's why you can see me."

Almost reflexively, Popcorn shut his blue eye, which wasn't, of course, funny-looking at all. But again, with his blue eye closed, Tiger disappeared. When it flew open, the ginger tom was back in place. In fact, if he closed his gold eye and looked at Tiger through the blue one alone, the old cat grew more solid.

Popcorn, on the other hand, wasn't feeling solid at all. His long slender legs were quaking so that he was having difficulty standing. He had always known his single blue eye made him *look* special, but he had never expected to *see* anything special with it, let alone a ghost!

Tiger was growing impatient. "I don't know who invited you here to see," he snarled. "It wasn't any of us, that's for sure."

"Any of *us*?" Popcorn repeated, looking around for the first time. He was as brave as the next cat, perhaps even braver than some, but he had never come up against a ghost before . . . at least not that he could recall. And if he had to see ghosts, one was more than enough.

As his glance flicked from one corner of the vestibule to the other, however, he discovered what Tiger meant by *us*. A Siamese floated in the doorway to the parlor, a long-haired calico sat perched on top of a nearby coatrack, and a black and white was stretched out sleepily on the ceiling. Every one of them was staring directly at him. By this time Popcorn didn't even have to close his blue eye to be certain what he was looking at. They were ghosts, every single one.

And without stopping to consider whether it was the best choice — or indeed, whether he had any choice at all — he turned and galloped up the stairs. He dashed into the room where he had been before and leapt to the windowsill, then stopped there, teetering, halfway through the hole in the screen.

How narrow the branch was! Popcorn looked back over his shoulder. All four cats had followed him, and they stood at the open door, peering into the room.

They looked merely curious, but even their curiosity had an uncanny feel about it, as though they were wondering how a white Cornish rex might taste. Popcorn took a deep breath and jumped.

For an instant he thought, *I'm flying!* and then, *I'm falling!* and then he was clinging to the slender branch. It was even less solid than it had looked. In fact, it dipped and swayed violently when he landed on it, then went on swaying with every small movement he made. Popcorn dug his claws in and hung on with all his might, nearly paralyzed with fright.

Behind him, he could hear the mewing

laughter of the ghost cats. Below him, the ground spun dizzily. He closed his eyes, both the gold and the blue, and took a long, quavering breath.

All I have to do now is climb down, he reminded himself. *Then I'm on my way to Portland. Or maybe I'll try Atlanta.*

But even as he said it, he knew he would never make it down from this terrible place. Not alive, anyway. And to his certain knowledge there was no such thing as a show for dead cats . . . in Boston or anywhere else.

What a wretched, awkward, embarrassing, totally undignified way to end his career. He couldn't let it happen. He just couldn't!

He opened his eyes, only a slit, but enough to get a glimpse of the ground again. Beneath the tree, close up to the trunk, a girl was huddled. His girl. The one who belonged to this house.

"Help!" he called. "You have to help me!"

But Melinda was sitting with her head buried in her arms, weeping, and for that moment, anyway, no one's misery was more urgent than her own.

5
The Release

POPCORN had been calling for a long time when Melinda finally lifted her head. She craned her neck to peer into the tree. Then she jumped to her feet.

It was a good thing spring had only just begun, that the leaves were still feathery and small. If the big oak had been fully leafed out, she never would have seen the skinny, white cat clinging to the high branch.

"Popcorn!" she called, and Popcorn replied with a long, mournful wail. The wail was so long and so mournful that the creature could have doubled as a foghorn on a foggy night.

"Hang on!" she yelled next.

Popcorn had every part of himself wrapped

around the branch, including his five-point tail. He muttered to himself, rather ungraciously for someone in his position, "Does the silly girl think I'm going to let go?" And then he added several other comments best not repeated here.

Fortunately, Melinda had no idea what he was saying. (It is probably just as well that humans *don't* understand cats. Their language can be quite rude.) She heard only pathetic-sounding mews that made her all the more determined to help. And so she jumped up, grabbed hold of the lowest branch, and pulled herself into the tree.

It was the kind of old tree that was perfect for climbing. And Melinda was the kind of girl who was accustomed to climbing trees. So, though it was very tall, she made her way easily, branch by branch.

Popcorn watched the girl moving toward him. The closer she got, the less certain he was that he wanted to be rescued . . . at least by her. Agents and judges always washed their hands, even sprayed them with disinfectant, before handling him. To be picked up by this wet-faced girl, to be clutched in her grimy hands . . . it was the final insult, really.

What cruel fate could have called him "home" to a world of unwashed children and ghost cats?

When Melinda's hands closed around him, Popcorn couldn't help himself. He clung to the limb even harder, despite the fact that he had expected to be marooned in this tree for the rest of his life. Drenched by the rain. Scorched by the sun. Starving and abandoned. Unseen and unappreciated.

"Come on, Popcorn," Melinda said softly. "It's all right. I'll take care of you."

There was something in the girl's voice that reminded Popcorn . . . Well, he wasn't exactly sure what it reminded him of, but it was pleasant, really. He loosed his hold, and when she lifted him into her arms, he clung as hard to her as he had to the branch.

Popcorn's claws penetrated Melinda's thin T-shirt, and she drew in her breath. She didn't pull him off, though. She had come to rescue him and rescue him she would. Besides, it felt rather good to have a cat clinging to her, de-

pending on her, even an ugly cat like this one. So she held him tenderly but firmly and made her way down.

It'll be nice to have a cat of my very own, she thought, brushing her cheek against his velvet fur. *Maybe I'll get used to the way he looks*.

Popcorn, however, wasn't planning on getting used to anything, especially a house filled with ghosts. The moment the girl reached the ground and started toward the front door, he began to struggle. When she squeezed him more tightly, he grabbed her arm with his claws to pull himself free.

"Oh!" Melinda cried out, dropping him into the grass. She held her stinging arm to examine the crisscross of red lines he had left.

Popcorn stood where he had fallen, stunned. How dare the girl *drop* him? Didn't she know anything about caring for a cat? He lifted first one paw, then another, from the unpleasantly tickly grass.

Melinda glared at him. She had never hurt an animal in her life, but she was half tempted to tweak this monster's tail. He was a cat who deserved to be annoyed.

Instead, she reached down to gather him into her arms again. However unpleasant he was, he belonged inside.

Popcorn hissed, and she straightened abruptly, changing her mind. "Look," she said, speaking brusquely to cover the tears choking her throat, "if you don't like it here, why don't you go? I don't care."

Popcorn couldn't believe his luck. The foolish girl was going to let him leave, just like that! He rippled his skin and took a couple of quick licks to rid himself of the last remnants of her touch, then asked, "Which way is Schenectady from here? I'm sure there'll be a show there."

But, of course, Melinda didn't understand his question any more than she had understood his earlier insults, and if she had understood, she would have been too miserable to answer anyway. Had there ever been a more unpleasant animal? Had there ever been a worse reason for moving?

She turned and plodded into the house, leaving Purrloom Popcorn alone in the middle of the front lawn.

A truck rumbled by on the street. In the distance, a gravel-voiced dog barked. Popcorn stood in the damp grass, unmoving. He gazed down the endless street, up at the distant sky, and all around at the unfamiliar world stretching away on every side. The scene couldn't have been more alien to him if he had just been released on Mars. He was overwhelmed and, there was no denying it, frightened.

It was the girl's fault, though. All of it. She hadn't even told him how to get to Salt Lake City from here!

Nonetheless, Purrloom Popcorn began walking.

6
The Reunion

POPCORN was running. He was fleeing, actually, moving so fast that his curly whiskers were blown straight in the wind. His long, slender legs sprang and coiled and sprang again. His tail streaked behind him like a white banner.

Still, the dog was gaining on him, bounding closer with every step, snapping at the tip of his tail.

Fortunately, each time the enormous teeth crashed closed, the dog missed by at least half an inch. Popcorn knew, however, that his luck — and his wind — were running out. And he also knew that if the beast ever caught him, more than his five-point tail would be in danger.

Who could have guessed that the world out-side of cat shows was such a terrible place? Since the girl had released him, he had been honked at, splashed with muddy water, threatened with a stick. And here he was, about to be eaten alive by a creature with more teeth than brains.

The dog had chased him around a corner, around another corner, across a street that he seemed to have crossed before. The houses were beginning to look faintly familiar, but then didn't all houses, like all humans, look pretty much alike?

Just ahead, a man was coming out a front door, his arms loaded with odds and ends. Popcorn took his chance. He charged up the stairs, bolted between the man's feet, and slid to a stop in the middle of the front vestibule.

The dog, of course, didn't follow. Cowards, all of them, the entire species.

The moment Popcorn was inside, however, the instant the door slammed shut behind him, he realized his mistake. Anything would have been a better choice than this. Perhaps it would have been better, even, to have stood and faced his pursuer. Because here he was, back inside the house that had held him captive before, and the ghost cats were still waiting for him.

Tiger sat on the curved end of the banister. The Siamese swirled in lazy circles about three feet off the floor as though caught in a gentle whirlpool in the air. The long-haired calico hung by her tail from the chandelier. The black and white was curled up, still half asleep, on a perfectly vertical wall. There was even a rotund Scottish fold he hadn't seen before, a rather clumsy ghost who seemed to be hung up in the wall halfway between the vestibule and the parlor.

Popcorn's gaze returned, inevitably, to the ginger tabby.

"So you're back," Tiger remarked. And then he added, gloating, "You ain't so purty anymore. Sweaty paws and a bit of dirt on your fur are an improvement, if you ask me."

Popcorn, of course, hadn't asked him, but before he could get his breath to say so, the Siamese floated between them. "Well, goodness me," she exclaimed, leaning down from her airy perch to peer into Popcorn's face. "Tiger, do you know who this is?"

"He's a breathing creature," Tiger replied, "one of *them*. His smell gives him away."

"Of course he smells," the Siamese agreed. "Breathing creatures do. But can't you see? He belongs here all the same."

The rest of the cats moved closer to see what she was talking about.

Popcorn was preparing an indignant reply on the subject of smell. Didn't he lick himself thoroughly many times a day? But he stopped when he found himself surrounded, almost exactly the way he used to be in shows. Except, of course, this was an audience of *ghosts*!

What could he do? There was no escape and, as he had already discovered, there were only horrors waiting for him outside anyway. The ghosts moved in even closer.

Popcorn looked from one to the other, then he took the only action that seemed to be left to him. He sank to the floor, curled into a tight ball, and covered his eyes, both of them, with his paws.

This was, without a doubt, the most terrible

day of his life. Torn from the work that he loved, ridiculed by children, marooned in trees, pursued by slathering hounds, tormented by ghosts! He had no strength for anything more.

The Siamese, however, went chattering on the way Siamese will. "Why, you've grown so," she was saying. "When I saw you earlier, I had no idea it was you. You were such a spidery kitten, you know. As a matter of fact, you were really quite odd-looking. Even odder than you are now, if you can believe that. You do remember us, don't you, Purrloom Popcorn?"

On hearing his name, Popcorn opened one eye. It happened to be the gold one, however, so he followed quickly with the blue. The only thing worse than seeing ghosts was hearing ghosts yet seeing nothing at all!

"You . . . you've heard about me then?" he asked in a wavering voice. It had never occurred to him that he might have admirers, even beyond his own world. A warm glow was traveling from his pink nose to the faraway tip of his tail, very much as it did when

47

a judge held him up to a crowd as the Best of the Best.

"Heard about you!" Tiger roared. "Why, knot my tail. I'm the one who taught you how to use a litter box!"

The warm glow turned into a sudden heat. Popcorn's ears pulsed with it. What a crude fellow this ginger tom was! And what was he talking about anyway?

"I taught you to play bat-the-mouse," the Siamese added. "Only once you'd learned, you began chasing ghost mice that none of us could see."

All the cats laughed, and Popcorn shuddered. He didn't know which repelled him more, the idea of playing with a ghost mouse or a live one. But he was beginning to get the picture. These cats knew nothing about his career. He had lived here with them once, when he was just a kitten . . . and when they, apparently, had been "breathing creatures," too.

He shuddered again.

The Scottish fold freed himself, finally, from the wall and lumbered over to announce,

"Twas I who taught you to lick every last drop of milk from your whiskers, laddie."

"And we taught you to twitch your tail and chatter at birds," the calico and the black and white said together. "Welcome home."

Home? Popcorn looked around, dazed. The way the light fell through the windows onto the patterned carpet, perhaps that *was* familiar. And there was a shadowy nook at the base of the stairs. Did he remember hiding there, pouncing on passing feet?

Still, even if this place had been his home, that didn't mean he had to come back. What was there here for him now? Dead cats? A girl with grimy hands?

A voice floated in from the other room. "And I'm the one who taught you how very special you are, Purrloom Popcorn."

Popcorn flicked his tail. Of course, he was special. No one had to teach him that. Still, he wanted to see who would make such an extravagant claim, and he stepped through the doorway into the parlor.

The parlor hadn't changed from when the

girl had released him there, except that his cage had been taken away (stolen, he supposed), and an empty rocking chair in the corner was swaying for no reason at all. Popcorn blinked and looked to the top of the tall, curved back of the chair.

An old woman was perched there, the oddest-looking old woman he had ever seen. She was wearing enormous, fuzzy slippers, a purple dress covered with large red and yellow flowers, and a green scarf, which floated around her neck. Her hair was in a proper enough white bun, but the bun floated, too, first to one side of her head, then to the other.

Popcorn gazed into the old woman's rumpled face, and his heart almost stopped beating.

Gentle hands, a warm lap, tidbits of fresh fish. They all came flooding back.

Was it . . . ? Could it be . . . ?

"Lydia." It was a word at first. Nothing more. Then he said it again, but softly, tentatively, like someone beginning a song while searching for the tune. "Lydia?"

"Of course, my dear," she replied. "Whom did you expect?"

Whom had he expected? Her. Only her. But then he had spent years expecting this woman, and she hadn't come. Years shuttling from show to show, looking for her, grieving for her. Because no one else, nothing else had ever mattered. Not the admiring crowds. Not the blue ribbons. Not even being on the cover of *The Distinctive Cat*.

It had been Lydia he had wanted, all along.

And yet he'd just been told something about her, something terrible. "Aren't you . . . aren't you . . . ?" he stammered. The word stuck in his throat.

"Dead?" she replied with a tinkling laugh. "Of course! And free, at last, to come home to all my dear cats."

Popcorn sat back on his haunches. He wrapped his tail around himself so tightly that it looped around his front ankles and formed a knot. And he stared at the beloved face. Stared and stared and stared.

It wasn't just that Lydia was a ghost. What was one more ghost in a house already filled with them? It was something else entirely, something he had always known but entirely forgotten.

His owner was special! Quite as special as he! For here she was, smiling back at him with one eye of golden brown and one of the softest, clearest blue.

7

The Promise

LYDIA had settled into the chair and gathered a lapful of cats. Only Popcorn remained on the floor, looking on with longing. Did he dare?

"I've been told, Popcorn," she was saying, "that you've won lots of blue ribbons."

"I have," he replied, quite modestly for him. And he wanted to add, but felt suddenly too shy, *I won them all for you.*

"You mean you've been kept in a cage, hauled around to shows?" the Siamese interrupted. She seemed horrified rather than impressed.

Popcorn ignored her. He was too intent

on Lydia's inviting lap to bother to explain that his cage was very comfortable, extremely secure, and that he certainly wasn't "hauled"; he was escorted from place to place.

"Do strangers stare at you?" someone asked.

"Why, yes, of course," Popcorn replied, impatient now. He had found the place he wanted. There was room, he was sure, on Lydia's right knee, next to the Scottish fold, whose name he'd found out was MacDougall.

"You mean you let humans stand in judgment about how you should look, the way you should behave?" someone else demanded to know.

In his heart, Popcorn was already curling into the soft warmth of that special spot. How well he could remember it now. But the questions kept pushing at him, aggravating him. "You don't seem to understand," he told them. "I was treated very well, kept comfortable and safe, fed the finest kitty kibbles." And then he added, since it was true,

55

"Never too much, of course. A gentleman on the show circuit has to watch his weight, you know."

They were all staring. It was clear they didn't understand. Not even Lydia, whose brown eye looked sorrowful and whose blue eye seemed almost teary.

"Were you lonely, Popcorn?" she asked. "Was it terribly hard? I'm sorry. I didn't mean for it to be so long until we were together again."

Had he been lonely? Popcorn sat very still. He'd been such a young kitten when Lydia had grown ill and sent him away. Loneliness had been like a constant itch beneath his skin, like a hunger for which there was no food.

But he wasn't going to admit such a thing in front of these self-satisfied spooks occupying the lap that was supposed to belong to him. They would think his whole life had been a sham. And it hadn't been. It had been a good life. A very distinguished life. He had the ribbons to prove it.

"No!" he exclaimed. "NO!! It was wonderful! It was fantastic! Why, I was Best of the Best! Everybody . . . why, just everybody loved me there!''

There was a long silence. Finally Tiger spoke. "Seems to me," he rumbled, "being loved by everybody ain't a whole lot better than being loved by nobody at all."

Popcorn wanted to cry. He might actually have done it except that white coats stain so easily, especially around the eyes.

He took a deep breath and tried, one last time, to explain. "They like my curly coat, don't you see? They give me five points for texture, ten for density, the full fifteen for waviness. They like my profile, too, and my large ears. And having one blue eye is considered very special. They give me ribbons for my blue eye."

"I have two blue eyes," the Siamese offered, "and —"

Lydia put her hand gently on the cat's head to silence her. To Popcorn she said, "There's so much that most folks never notice. It's quite wonderful what you can see with one blue eye, don't you agree?"

Did he? Popcorn had never given much thought to what he saw, only to being seen. But because she had said it was wonderful, he closed his gold eye, just experimentally, and studied Lydia and the other cats through the blue.

The first thing he noticed was that they all were solid, quite as solid as he. But there was more, much more. Because looking carefully through his ghost eye, Popcorn could see that Tiger, for all his bluster, was very unsure of himself. That the Siamese wanted to be noticed. That the black and white and the calico both missed their many kittens who'd been sent off into the world. That MacDougall had been hungry as a small kitten, and he was hungry still, no matter how much he'd just eaten. And that Lydia, Lydia of the cheerfully wild dress, had been lonely herself for a long, long time.

Seeing them all, really seeing them, Popcorn remembered something more. He remembered that they had loved him, every one. Even more important, that *he* had loved *them*.

And filled with that love, filled with the memory of the games they had played, the food they had shared, of Lydia's gentle hands stroking his fur, tickling his whiskers, he took a deep breath and leapt up to join his friends on the lap that had waited so long for him.

Only, of course, there was no place for him there anymore, couldn't possibly be, no matter how deep his longing. For when Popcorn landed, his paws went right through the translucent flowers in Lydia's dress, through her legs, even through two of the other cats, to the chair itself. They all swirled around him like a cool though colorful fog. And he stood alone on the chair.

"Oh!" he cried. "Oh my!" And he scrambled down even more quickly than he had jumped up.

Lydia and the other cats looked on sadly.

What good did it do to have a ghost eye, to see into a world he couldn't touch? What good did it do to come home, for that matter, when everyone he had ever loved was dead?

"It's no use," he cried. "No use at all. I can't stay here, don't you see? I don't belong with you anymore."

"Belong with us?" Lydia cried. "Why, of course you do."

The cats, most of them anyway, mewed their agreement.

Popcorn shook his head. "You're very kind, but a breathing creature has no place among ghosts. Surely you know that."

"He's right!" Tiger announced. "Absolutely right."

Popcorn couldn't help but wish that Tiger had found some other subject on which to agree with him so emphatically, but still he nodded his thanks to the old tabby. "I'm a show cat now. It's the only thing I know, the only thing I'm good at. I need to go back there."

"Are you sure?" Lydia leaned forward earnestly, but even as she spoke she was floating upwards from her chair. The lapful of ghost cats, of course, floated with her. "Were you happy there?"

"Yes," Popcorn replied. "Yes!" Happier than he could be here, anyway. Besides, what other choice did he have? And when Lydia continued to rise toward the ceiling — was she abandoning him again? — he called after her loudly, "Lydia, please! You've got to help me."

"Help you?" she replied. "Help you!" she repeated, bumping against the ceiling like a released helium balloon. "Of course, we'll help you. Won't we, darlings?"

She turned a somersault, and cats floated out of her lap in every direction. They settled gently on the floor all around Popcorn like large and oddly colored snowflakes.

"We will," they agreed. Even Tiger said it, more loudly than all the rest.

"You were our friend when you were but a wee lad," MacDougall reminded Popcorn.

Popcorn wanted to reply, but his throat was so tight he couldn't say anything at all. Instead, he stood and took a brief turn in the middle of the floor, as though he were on the judge's table.

It was a kind of bow and the only way he knew to thank her, to thank them all.

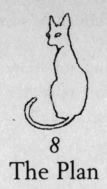

8
The Plan

THE plan was in place. It was sure to work. The cats, led by Popcorn, would create a nuisance. Enough of a nuisance that, as Tiger announced — a bit more enthusiastically than was entirely necessary, Popcorn thought — "They'll be glad to see the last of your skinny tail."

Lydia said that she, in the meantime, would talk to each of the family members in turn. She would explain that Popcorn was a valuable cat, a show cat after all, and that he should be returned to the show circuit.

"Of course, they won't understand me exactly," she added, "but they'll hear me all the same. People always assume that ghosts' voices are merely their own thoughts."

"That's good," the Siamese said. "In my experience humans always obey better when they think they're in charge."

Lydia, who, of course, had been the Siamese's human, looked startled. The other cats laughed.

"Shhh!" the calico said. "Shhhhh!" And they all fell silent, listening. They could hear the family gathering in the kitchen for supper.

"Now," MacDougall whispered, "it's time to begin." And they headed for the kitchen. Popcorn, followed by MacDougall and the Siamese, jumped up onto the kitchen table and cruised across, sampling this and that on his way by.

"Is that Great-aunt Lydia's cat?" Melinda's mother asked, staring at Popcorn. She had one hand over the butter dish and the other protecting her own plate.

"Yes," Melinda said. "It's Purrloom Popcorn." She was surprised to see him inside again, but not especially interested in how he'd gotten there. He was, after all, a thoroughly unsatisfactory cat.

"Not very attractive, is he?" her mother said in a doubtful voice.

Just then, a glass of iced tea that had been sitting solidly on the table tipped into Mother's lap. Startled and confused, unable to make out the ghostly Siamese behind the spill, she glared at Popcorn and grabbed for a napkin to mop up.

MacDougall knocked the lid off the sugar bowl. The family saw no one except Popcorn, who sauntered over, tested the sugar with one perfect oval paw, then began scratching as though he had found a litter box. Father's face grew red.

"Get that cat!" he ordered, glaring at Melinda as though Popcorn's very existence were, somehow, her fault.

Melinda didn't move. Aside from the fact that she didn't want to risk getting scratched again, she was quite enjoying her parents' dilemma. Hadn't they been the ones who'd been so pleased over Great-aunt Lydia's will?

"Send Popcorn to the nearest cat show," Lydia whispered into Melinda's ear, then she swung across the table on the hanging light fixture and repeated the order to Melinda's father.

Popcorn jumped up to Mother's shoulder

and launched himself in the direction of the sink.

"Send Popcorn back to his agent," Lydia repeated to Mother, who was rubbing her shoulder where Popcorn's claws had pricked through her blouse.

"He *is* our responsibility," Mother said to no one in particular. "After all, he was Great-aunt Lydia's cat." She seemed to be arguing with her own thoughts . . . or with what she assumed were her own thoughts.

"It's only right that we take him in," Father agreed.

Take him in? As if he were some kind of stray! Popcorn knocked a spoon into the garbage disposal. Another ghost cat, a blue-gray he hadn't seen before, hit the switch.

"Get it!" Father yelled, and as Mother lunged to turn off the grinding racket, the black and white cat tripped her.

Tiger, in the meantime, had left a phantom "gift" in the middle of the kitchen floor. It couldn't be seen, but it surely did smell.

Melinda's mother picked herself up and turned off the switch. "You know," she said, sinking into her chair again and sniffing, "I've scrubbed this floor a dozen times, and I can still smell that old woman's cats."

Lydia, who had been an excellent housekeeper before she'd grown ill and whose house had *never* smelled of cats, grew angry. Forgetting their careful plan, she jumped up on top of the table and yelled at the top of her lungs, "Send Popcorn anywhere, everywhere! Just send him back! Not one of you deserves a cat!"

"You know," Mother spoke slowly, like someone exploring a new and rather astonishing idea, "we could send him away. He's only a cat, after all. One place must be as good as another to him."

Popcorn had jumped to the top of the refrigerator, and he looked down, astonished. What did these people think he was, anyway, some dumb dog to be shunted from place to place? And not to know? Still, he mustn't complain. The woman was moving in the right direction.

Father rubbed his shin where the calico had been sharpening her ghostly claws. "Lydia *is*

dead," he reminded them all in his most reasonable voice.

"You're right, dearie. Dead as a doorknob,
and I'd never, ever know," Great-aunt Lydia
chortled, patting his rather bald head so that
he stopped rubbing his shin and began rubbing
his scalp instead.

"But it's up to Melinda, really," her mother
said. "I know you've always longed for a cat.
Do *you* want to keep him, dear?"

Popcorn held his breath, watching Melinda
intently. She would want to keep him, of
course. She was going to spoil everything by
wanting him to stay.

However, Melinda shook her head. "No,"
she told her parents, not even bothering to
look in Popcorn's direction. "I don't want
him. He's the rudest, ugliest cat I've ever seen.
I don't think he even knows how to be a cat."

What? I don't know what? Popcorn almost
fell off the top of the refrigerator. How could
she say such a thing about the holder of un-
counted blue ribbons, a Grand Champion, the
Best of the Best? How could she even think
such a thing about *him*?

And where was her loyalty, anyway? Wasn't this the child who always longed for a cat? Of course he wanted to leave. There was no question about that. But still it was a rude blow to discover that these people — especially the girl — wanted him to leave, too.

Well, if that's the way it's going to be, I might as well give them good reason, he said to himself. And that was when he flung himself from the refrigerator onto Melinda's father's head. Naturally, once he landed he had to dig in his claws to keep his perch.

"Get him off!" Father yelled. "Off!"

"Send him back!" Lydia cried. "Back!"

"That's enough!" Mother cried. "I've never seen such a terrible cat in my entire life. He has to go!"

"But where will we send him?" Father asked, after Mother had grabbed Popcorn and deposited him, none-too-gently, on the floor.

"To the nearest cat show!" Lydia cried triumphantly.

"To the pound," Melinda's mother said.

There was a stunned silence in the room. Popcorn stood frozen where he had been put down. Lydia and the ghost cats sank slowly, almost solidly to the floor. Even Melinda drew in a horrified breath. Was this what she had wanted? Was it?

But it didn't matter whether it was or not, because her mother repeated emphatically, in that tone parents use when their minds are entirely made up, "It's too late to do anything tonight. But first thing tomorrow, we're going to take this wretched cat to the pound."

9

The Beginning

It was late at night, and Lydia sat in the rocking chair in the middle of the dark parlor. The ghost cats were curled in her lap, draped across her shoulders; one was even perched on her head. Popcorn sat on the floor surrounded by cats as well. Two or three more had come in since the kitchen fiasco. He had lost count.

"I was giving the wrong message," Lydia moaned for the thousandth time. "I should have been more specific. 'Send him to the nearest cat show! Send him to the nearest cat show!' I should have kept saying that."

"It doesn't have the same ring, somehow,"

Popcorn pointed out. There was, after all, nothing to be gained by regret.

Lydia gazed at Popcorn. Her eyes were bright with ghostly tears. "I tried to explain, after they said that dreadful word . . ."

"Pound," Tiger repeated glumly.

The Siamese shuddered. "Don't!" And they all fell silent.

After a time Lydia spoke again. "They just won't listen. I've been up there half the night" — she glanced toward the stairs — "talking to them in their sleep. But they don't hear me. I'm sure they don't hear me."

She reached down and passed her hand along Popcorn's back. He could almost feel her touch. It wasn't like being petted exactly, not at all like his comforting memories, vague as they were. Her hand was more like a breath of cool air along his spine. "Someone nice will adopt you," she promised. "You're special, you know."

Popcorn shook his head. "You think all your cats are special," he said. "But most people don't have a ghost eye to see it the way you do."

"Or you," Lydia said, but Popcorn only shook his head again.

He might have *looked* through his blue eye, but he hadn't *seen*. Mostly he had just sat around while people looked at him, the way they were going to be looking at him in the pound. He had heard rumors about what happened to the animals at the pound, the ones no one chose. Without all his ribbons to prove that he was supposed to be special, would anyone want him? Was there any reason that they should?

He, himself, had never cared about another living creature . . . except, perhaps, for Lydia and the rest of her cats, and that had been too long ago to count. All babies cared about those who cared for them.

Popcorn stood up, his tail hanging limp. It was too late to alter his fate, but he hated to think that he had ruined the girl, made it so she would never want another cat. "I think I'll go upstairs," he said, "just check on things, you know?"

No one could think of anything better to do while they waited for morning, so they all nodded.

Popcorn climbed the stairs, pushed through the door into the now-familiar room, and jumped onto the windowsill again. The night smelled of earth and of new, green growth, but he turned his attention to the inside.

The first thing he saw was that the girl had put all his ribbons on the wall above her bed, his whole career on display. He hadn't noticed that when he'd been in the room before. He stared at them for a long time. There weren't so many, really. And it was strange, but if he looked at the ribbons through his blue eye, they seemed, almost, to disappear.

The girl was sleeping, curled into an awkward looking S. The stuffed cat had fallen from her arms and was lying on the floor, its red eyes staring. Popcorn wondered what a cat could see through red eyes.

Then he noticed something else. The girl

had set his cage, the one he had arrived in, in the corner. There was even fresh water in a bowl, kibbles in another. She had lined his cage with a doll blanket for extra softness, too.

He considered jumping down for some kibbles and a bit of cool water, but then he didn't. He'd be back behind bars soon enough anyway.

The idea that the girl had done all that for him touched him, though. It made him remember that she had climbed up and rescued him from the tree. And she hadn't forced him to come inside when he had wanted to stay out, either. Popcorn jumped over to the bed to examine her more closely.

Through his gold eye he saw that she was really quite pretty. Her skin was golden. Her lashes lay like thick brushes against her cheeks. Her lips, though turned down at the corners, were soft and full.

And through his blue eye he saw that, besides being pretty, she was frightened and lonely and sad.

He tiptoed toward her pillow. She had been crying, and the tears had dried, leaving streaks of crusted salt on her cheeks. He didn't need his ghost eye to see that.

Maybe he didn't need his ghost eye anyway. Maybe, all along, he could have seen everything that mattered if he'd only bothered to look.

Seems to me, being loved by everybody ain't a whole lot better than being loved by nobody at all. That was Tiger, the rough old cob. Where did he come off, talking about love?

Popcorn licked away a bit of the salt from the girl's cheek. She stirred.

She might have been an ally if he had treated her differently.

The girl's eyelids fluttered, came open, and Popcorn drew back. But then he saw that she was pulling back as well. She was afraid, poor thing . . . of him!

"It's all right, little one," he said in his softest voice. "I won't hurt you."

And though he knew she couldn't understand, she seemed, somehow, to know that he meant to be friendly. She held a hand, very cautiously, toward him.

Popcorn rose to meet the hand, and she stroked the length of his back, all the way to the tip of his tail. Then she did it again.

The judges had always held him gently. His agents had groomed him and fed him and treated him well in all ways. He was too valuable to be treated badly. But no one, not even Lydia, had ever touched him with such trembling fear and hope.

Or with such wistful love.

Popcorn trembled, too. Was it possible that there was still a chance? For both of them? He had waited so long for the old woman, and she hadn't returned, had been unable to return, but now . . .

"Come, Popcorn," the girl said. "Come to Melinda."

So . . . his girl had a name. He supposed he had heard it before, but he hadn't been paying attention.

Popcorn moved closer and settled next

to Melinda, tucking his paws beneath his chest.

Cautiously, she wrapped an arm around the beautiful, white cat. "I won't let them take you away," she said, touching his curling whiskers.

Popcorn began to purr.

Melinda smiled. She might have been smiling at the wisp of an old woman hovering over the bed or at the ghostly cats dancing around her, but she wasn't. She was smiling at Popcorn.

"There's a cat show right here in Chicago," Lydia murmured, bending close to Melinda's ear. "Wouldn't you like to enter Purrloom Popcorn?"

But Melinda didn't seem to hear, and Popcorn, nestled into the curve of her arm, didn't especially care.

Lydia stirred her grandniece's curls with ghostly fingers and smiled, too. There would be lots of time to talk to Melinda, lots to teach her about cats. There was no hurry.

Lydia and the ghost cats each found a place

and settled around the bed so gently that they didn't even rumple a cover. Popcorn turned his head slowly, carefully, and winked his blue eye at them all, just once. Then he tucked his perfect, pink nose beneath Melinda's chin, and he and Melinda slept.

MARION DANE BAUER lives in Eden Prairie, Minnesota, where she and her friend breed Cornish rex and Devon rex kittens. "Purrloom Popcorn is, in fact, based on our own Purrloom Popcorn, with a few important differences. Our Popcorn is a she, she has never lived in a cage, and has two gold eyes. I'm confident, however, that our Popcorn *does* see ghosts!"

Ms. Bauer writes full-time, and is the author of ten distinguished books for young people including *Shelter from the Wind*, *Rain of Fire*, and her 1987 Newbery Honor book, *On My Honor*.

TRINA SCHART HYMAN, who began as a printmaker, really enjoyed illustrating *Ghost Eye* in black-and-white line art. "I found it a complete challenge," she said, "to make the Cornish rex, an unbelievably hideous-looking animal, charming and appealing." Ms. Hyman, illustrator of over 140 books for children, was awarded the Caldecott Medal for *St. George and the Dragon*, and both *Little Red Riding Hood* and *Hershel and the Hanukkah Goblins* were named Caldecott Honor books. She lives in a 182-year-old farmhouse in Lyme, New Hampshire, where she is raising varying numbers of cats, two dogs, and three sheep.